Toni's
TOPSY - TURVY
Telephone
Day

Laura
Ljungkvist

ams, Inc., Publishers

Toni loved to throw parties. One day she decided to have a dinner party. A potluck dinner party. She planned everything down to the last detail. Then she called her friends to invite them and to tell them what to bring.

The first person Toni called
was cousin Ruth. Ruth lived next
to the airport. Toni asked her to
bring punch and lemonade to
the party.

Next, Toni called Frank. He was listening to his favorite radio station. Toni asked Frank to bring bread and cheese.

Then Toni called Vera. Vera was a professional dogwalker. Toni asked her to bring a steak to kabob to the dinner party.

When Toni called Otto, he was watching his favorite TV show. She asked Otto to bring a strawberry pie.

Toni then telephoned Kirk, who was babysitting. She asked him to bring hats and balloons to the party.

Fiona lived next to the fire
station. Toni called and asked
her to bring salad and juice.

Toni was very busy before the arrival of her dinner guests. First there was the job of picking out a chic dress with shoes to match. She had to decide on jewelry and perfume. Then she had to paint her toenails and style her hair. Toni was just about to start setting the table when the doorbell rang. Her first guest!

"Hello, Ruth . . . Oh, no! I asked you to bring punch and lemonade, not a pooch and a maid!"

"Frank, hello . . . Oh, no! I asked for bread and cheese, not a bride and your niece!"

"Hello, Vera . . . Oh, no! I asked for a steak to kabob, not a snake and a snob!"

"Hello, Otto . . . Oh, no! I said to bring a strawberry pie, not a stranger and a spy!"

"Kirk, hello . . . Oh, no! Hats and balloons, not cats and baboons!"

"Hello, Fiona . . . Oh, no! Salad and juice, not a sailor and a moose!"

Instead of food, Toni's friends had all brought more guests to the party. And everyone looked really hungry. All Toni had in the house was a can of tuna and two clementines. Certainly not enough to feed this crowd!

What was Toni to do? While the guests got acquainted, Toni racked her brain. Suddenly, she had an idea . . .

Pizza! Of course! Everybody likes pizza! When Toni called the pizza parlor, the party was so noisy that Toni had to shout her order: "A superlarge pizza with extra cheese, please!"

A little while later the doorbell rang. Soon the hungry crowd would be fed, Toni thought.

"Hello . . . Oh, no! Pizza with extra cheese, not pizza with eggs and bees!" What was poor Toni to do now?

Before Toni could say "clementine," the eggs hatched. And the birds and bees, who all turned out to be very friendly, joined the party. Toni sliced the pizza and it was munched down by the happy crowd.

The moon and stars kept Toni company when the last guest had left. The party had been a fabulous success! Everyone made new friends and no one left hungry. Toni was very happy. As she was getting ready for bed, the telephone rang. It was one of her new friends inviting her to a dinner party.

"Oh, yes, I would love to come,"
Toni said. "May I bring something?"

Acknowledgments

The completion of this book marks the end of a road with many twists and turns.
My sincere thanks to those who helped and believed in me along the way. – L. L.

Artist's Note

I sketch with a fine marker on drafting paper. By sketching on different pieces of this translucent paper
and cutting and pasting them on top of each other, I can alter each image without creating an entirely
new sketch. When I am happy with my sketches, I use a lightbox and a pencil to transfer them to watercolor
paper. Then it's time to paint! I use Winsor & Newton gouache paint. I save the colors I mix in small plastic
containers, labeling all the containers with a small painted sample. When I worked on this book, I wrote
the name of the character to which each color belonged on the corresponding container. Now Toni
and her friends can pop up in a number of my illustrations, even if only in color!
– Laura Ljungkvist

The art is gouache on paper.
This book is set in 20 point Gill Sans
Designer: Edward Miller

Library of Congress Cataloging-in-Publication Data

Ljungkvist, Laura.

Toni's topsy-turvy telephone day / written and illustrated
by Laura Ljungkvist.
p. cm.
Summary: Toni decides to have a potluck dinner party and calls each of her friends to
bring an item, but because of background noise, they each bring the wrong thing!
ISBN 0–8109–4486–3
[1. Parties—Fiction. 2. Dinners and dining—Fiction. 3. Humorous stories.] I. Title.

PZ7.L7657 To 2001
[E]—dc21   00–42154

Copyright © 2001 Laura Ljungkvist

Published in 2001 by Harry N. Abrams, Incorporated, New York

Printed and bound in Hong Kong

Harry N. Abrams, Inc.
100 Fifth Avenue
New York, N.Y. 10011
www.abramsbooks.com